"And the Lord God formed man of the dust of the ground, and breathed into his nostrils the breath of life; and man became a living soul."

GENESIS 2:7

CLAY MAN

Clay Man

THE GOLEM OF PRAGUE

A Retelling by IRENE N. WATTS
Illustrated by KATHYRN E. SHOEMAKER

TUNDRA BOOKS

Published in Canada by Tundra Books,
75 Sherbourne Street, Toronto, Ontario M5A 2P9

Published in the United States by Tundra Books of Northern New York,
P.O. Box 1030, Plattsburgh, New York 12901

Library of Congress Control Number: 2008910106

LIBRARY AND ARCHIVES CANADA
CATALOGUING IN PUBLICATION

Watts, Irene N., 1931-
Clay man : the Golem of Prague / Irene N. Watts ; Kathryn E.
Shoemaker, illustrator.

ISBN 978-0-88776-880-4

1. Golem – Juvenile fiction. I. Shoemaker, Kathryn E. II. Title.
PS8595.A873C49 2009   jC813'.54   C2008-907124-7

We acknowledge the financial support of the Government of Canada through the Book
Publishing Industry Development Program (BPIDP) and that of the Government of
Ontario through the Ontario Media Development Corporation's Ontario Book
Initiative. We further acknowledge the support of the Canada Council for the Arts
and the Ontario Arts Council for our publishing program.

ONTARIO ARTS COUNCIL
CONSEIL DES ARTS DE L'ONTARIO

DESIGN: CS RICHARDSON

Printed in Canada

1 2 3 4 5 6   14 13 12 11 10 09

For Tania and Jean-Michel Gariépy

– i.n.w.

For Hannah Everett,

a gifted storyteller – k.e.s.

⊰━━⊱

*My continuing thanks to Kathy Lowinger and Sue Tate,
and to Sarah Duncan for advice.*

CONTENTS

Before   XI

1. Ghetto   1
2. Passover   7
3. "I must make a golem"   11
4. "This is the place"   17
5. Clay Man   21
6. Josef   27
7. "Not like other men"   31
8. "No smoke without fire"   37
9. A Wedding Feast   43
10. "Poison"   49
11. The Blood Lie   55
12. "To save a life"   63
13. "He is only sleeping"   71
14. "The courage to speak"   77

Afterword   83

BEFORE

I am of clay
Old as earth
I lie here
Waiting
River washes over me
Water cools me, Sun warms me
I know light and dark
Light is bright and dark is black
I lie and wait

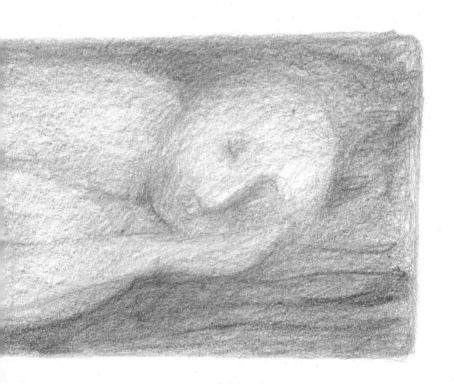

1. GHETTO

Father says that Prague is the most beautiful city in the world. We live in the small part of the city, in the ghetto, which is also called the Jewish town. We are surrounded by walls. Five hundred Jews live here, inside the walled town. We must wear a yellow circle on our clothes to show who we are.

Merchants, tradesmen, and those who come to the market square from other quarters of Prague to buy and sell and look for bargains can wear whatever they like.

Our houses are crooked, crammed close together with no space between. When a voice is raised, or a baby cries, everyone in the street can hear what is happening. Sometimes I forget about being quiet and slam the door of my room. (I have a room to myself now that my brother, Shimon, has gone away to study.)

When I make a noise, Father looks at me, shakes his head, and says, "Jacob, must I remind you again that I have work to do?"

Mother hustles me away, sighing. "Do you think this is how Shimon behaved?"

My older brother lives in Vienna, with a rabbi and his family. He attends the *yeshiva* there, the school of higher learning. One day he, too, will become a rabbi, like Father.

Emperor Rudolf, who rules all of Bohemia, comes from Vienna. Now he lives here, in a castle on a hilltop. From there, Father says, he looks over all of Prague – its bridges, spires, domes, and the mighty Vltava, the river that flows through the golden city.

Father says the emperor is our friend because he permits us to live in the Jewish town. He does not banish us to wander homeless around the world. He wants all of his citizens to live peacefully, side by side.

The gates of our ghetto are locked at night to keep us safe. No one comes in and no one goes out. Even our dead are buried inside the walls of the town. I want so much to go outside the ghetto . . . to see the wonders of the city that everyone talks about.

Mother says all we need is right here: the synagogues in which we worship, schools, markets, and our fine town hall with its Hebrew clock.

"What need is there to leave the Jewish quarter?" she says. "Here, there is safety – why walk among strangers? We have our own merchants, goldsmiths, butchers, shoemakers, innkeepers, tailors, a doctor, an astronomer and an astrologist, teachers, and many learned men. Be content."

My father, Rabbi Judah Loew, is the most learned of them all. He is a great teacher, a wise man known all over the city and even across Bohemia and the lands beyond. He reads and prays, day and night. No problem is too hard for him to solve.

Everyone seeks his advice. He understands many languages and writes books too. One day, I hear a story about him in the marketplace:

Years ago, long before I was born, there was a great plague. Hundreds of people in Prague died, but my father encountered the skeletal figure of Death in the cemetery.

The story people tell is, he showed no fear, but argued for the Jews of the ghetto. He pleaded for each name that Death had written on a list, held in his bony fingers.

When the plague was over, nearly all the Jews of the ghetto had been spared.

Some say Father has great powers . . . that he is a magician. When we walk home together after the service in the synagogue, people stop him and praise his sermon. Then they turn to me.

I wait, dreading the question they always ask.

"So, Jacob, will you grow up to be a great teacher like your father?"

I look at the ground, searching for words. *How can I tell them that I don't like to study, that the Hebrew letters blur on the page, and that my thoughts wander?*

Does no one understand how hard it is to be the son of a famous rabbi? Worse, to be the younger brother of Shimon, who has always loved learning?

I want to go outside the ghetto gates, explore the fine streets and squares, run across bridges, swim in the river, and climb up the hill to the castle. I hear that in one of the castle towers, astronomers watch the sky day and night through a special instrument.

From my bedroom window, I see only a patch of sky – the rest is hidden by the walls that shut us in. *Does the sky look bigger away from our narrow alleys, gloomy courtyards, and crooked lanes?*

Why do the clouds change shape? What makes the sun and moon and stars appear and disappear? What causes the tides to ebb and flow? How is the world put together? I want to find out. Will the ancient texts we read day after day help me do that? One day, I will go and find the answers to all my questions.

2. PASSOVER

Winter will soon be over. I long for spring. In March, we celebrate Passover. Each year, as the youngest son, I ask the question, "Why is this night different from all other nights?"

Father tells the story of how our ancestors left Egypt to wander in the wilderness. Anything was better than staying in Egypt, where they had been slaves. Finally, after many, many years, Pharaoh, the ruler, agreed to let them go.

This is the first year for Rebecca, my baby sister, to hear the story. She listens, watching Father, for once not grabbing at his beard!

"Pharaoh had broken his promise to our people many times. Would he change his mind again? The Jews were anxious to begin their journey. They feared that mighty Pharaoh would order his guards to prevent them, his Jewish slaves, from leaving and force them to stay in Egypt. They knew they must hurry away.

"The baking was not ready. What was to be done?

They needed food for the journey. They took the bread out of the ovens before it had time to rise. This is why we eat unleavened bread, matzos, *during Passover. On this festival, we remind ourselves of the difficulties our people had to overcome."*

For most of the year, we live in peace with our neighbors on the other side of the wall. But Christians celebrate their Easter festival around the same time as we do Passover, and we are anxious. This is a dangerous time to be a Jew.

The people from outside spread lies and accuse us of dreadful deeds. They stand at the gates of the ghetto, raising their fists and voices against us. Their words give me bad dreams, even though I will soon be ten years old.

Father says it is only a few ignorant people who spread the "Blood Lie." It is how they attack what they do not understand.

No one knows when the lie started, Father says, but it has plagued Jews for centuries. Every year at this time, the people accuse us of killing Christian children, of mixing our matzos with their blood.

THIS EVENING, elders from our congregation come to the house to talk with Father. I am sent to bed. Voices are raised, and I overhear some of what they say.

"Read the *Torah* – in the words of our bible lies our defense," Father says.

"But who can tell how far our enemies will go to prove the Blood Lie?" an elder asks.

"The emperor does not allow us weapons. What can we do to defend ourselves when they threaten to burn our synagogues, Rabbi?"

"Not even the land upon which our houses stand is our own, and yet they begrudge us our very homes."

The elders are afraid and so am I!

"Emperor Rudolf may not protect us forever, Rabbi. What then?"

"He is a wise ruler. The people listen to him. He will calm their fears. After all, this is the year 1590 – we no longer live in the Dark Ages. I will pray for guidance. Go to your homes and do the same. All will be well," Father says.

I hear them thanking him. Father will find a way to let us welcome Passover safely. Nothing bad will happen, and I am comforted.

3. "I MUST MAKE A GOLEM"

After the elders leave, I wait. I do not want to disturb Father at his prayers. When all is quiet, I knock on his study door, as I do every night before I go to sleep. He keeps these few minutes for me only.

He tells me to come in. I stand beside him and read the title of the book that is open in front of him. I have heard my teacher mention it – the *Sefer Yezirah* – a book of mystical writings about the Creation, too difficult for all but the most learned men, scholars of *kabbala*, to understand.

"There is great wisdom in these pages, Jacob. I am seeking answers that remain hidden from me. I hope, through study and prayer, that all will be revealed. The truth is not easy to find."

"What is hidden from you, Father? What kind of truth?"

"Jacob, can you tell me how the world was created?" It is Father's way – to reply to a question with another.

For once I know the answer: "God commanded it, Father."

"How did He command it?"

"He said, 'Let there be light: and there was light.'"

"Good. He commanded the world into being with the power of his words."

Then Father asks another question: "How are words formed, Jacob?" I hope I have the answer to this one too.

"With the twenty-two letters of the Hebrew alphabet, written and read from right to left." When one has a rabbi for a father, everything is a lesson!

"You will yet become a scholar like your brother. That is correct. Our Hebrew alphabet contains the holy name of the Creator. By arranging and rearranging the letters of the alphabet, I pray that the solution to the dangers that face us will be revealed to me." Father bends over the pages of the book. I say good night and leave him to his reading.

Before I go to sleep, I tell myself that one day I will be brave enough to confess to Father that I don't want the same things as Shimon. I am afraid of disappointing him.

In my dream, I walk outside the ghetto, along the bank of the river Vltava, as I have wanted to do for so long.

I stop to plunge my hands in the water. Red clay oozes between my fingers. I grab big handfuls – enough to sculpt something splendid. I knead and shape, without planning

what the clay will become. A head forms in my hands.
Will it become the head of a fierce lion, with a mane? Our
family name, Loew, means lion. But this does not look like
a beast — it resembles the head of a giant man. I continue
to work, molding the neck and shoulders. I will make him
taller even than Shimon.

I am so busy with my task that I do not notice the tide creeping in until my feet are covered by swirls of dark water. When it recedes, the shape has disappeared, taken back by the river. I am left alone on the bank. Nothing remains of what I made.

Father's cry wakes me – I run to him! His study door is open, the candle flickering beside him. *Who is Father talking to?*

"I must make a *golem*, create him of earth, fire, water, and air . . . a golem to protect us from our enemies. . . . Who is there?"

"Jacob, Father. I was dreaming. I woke up when you called out."

"What was your dream?" Father's hand rests on the open pages of the *Sefer Yezirah*. He shuts the book.

"I played by the river and I made a shape from clay."

"What kind of shape?" Father asks harshly. *Is he angry with me?* His eyes gaze into mine as if I have done something wrong.

"It was only a dream, Father. I did not really leave the ghetto. The water came and washed away what I made. I don't remember."

Father puts his hand on my head in a gesture of blessing. "It is not yet day. Go back to bed, my son."

I do as I'm told, but his whisper follows me: "It is the same, the same dream."

I lie awake until dawn. *How can we both dream the same dream? I was only playing with clay – why would my father, the great rabbi, dream of such childish things?*

4. "This is the place"

All week, Father's study door remains shut. No one is allowed to disturb him. He does not come into the kitchen for meals. Mother says he is fasting – rabbis fast even more often than ordinary men.

Seven nights after my dream of the river, I hear noises in the night. Father's door creaks as it opens and closes. I recognize his tread on the stairs. Quietly, so as not to wake my mother and the baby, I follow him outside, but he has vanished.

It is the darkest part of the night, when shapes and shadows, spirits and demons haunt the ghetto.

A rat skitters across the slippery cobblestones – he is braver and more used to the darkness than I am. Then a sliver of moon appears, and I no longer wish I had not come. I see Father and two men walking ahead of me. They wear white garments, clothes kept for Holy Days. *Are they going to the synagogue to pray?* I watch them glide through the uneven streets like ghosts.

The thought makes me shiver, so I hurry not to be

too far behind them. I keep close to the shuttered houses. Father pauses to confer with his companions. So as not to be noticed, I try to breathe softly and cover my face with my sleeve until they move on.

There is just enough light for me to recognize the stooped shoulders of Isaac, Father's most trusted student. He carries a bundle. The other man, walking beside him, is Samuel – the husband of my older sister, Devora. The town hall clock sounds the hour, three times.

The moon disappears again, for a mist shrouds the ghetto in these fearful hours before dawn. *Why has Father not lit the torches they have brought with them?* Everyone knows that fire keeps away evil creatures.

They pass the Old-New Synagogue and approach the cemetery, whose crooked tombstones startle me, looming out of the gloom, leaning and swaying in the dark like old men at prayer.

Soon Father and his companions reach the gates of the ghetto. I begin to call out, but stifle my cry. I know that Father would send me home. He unlocks the gates, passes through, and locks them again. I press my face against the barrier, afraid to lose sight of the three men. *How can I follow now?*

Then I remember that further down, where the walls do not quite meet, the stones have crumbled. My fingers feel their way to the opening, no wider

than the span of a man's hand. I push through
sideways, ignoring the rough edges scraping at my
clothes. *Are they trying to hold me back?* Except in my
dreams, I have never been outside the ghetto walls.

The moon emerges once more, and the light
changes the men's white garments to blue. They
walk more quickly now, lengthening the distance
between us.

I have no time to admire the fine houses with
their beautifully painted signs and numbers; ours
have none. Here the streets are broader and cleaner,
and they do not smell of herring and onions like ours
do. I almost wish I was home again.

We leave the city behind. Father disappears into
a small wooded grove, and the others follow. I hear
them stumbling over roots and through brambles. I
smell the river . . . hear it rushing by. The winter ice
has melted.

Ahead is a clearing. Now I become a shadow,
twisting and turning among the gnarled branches.
I find a low thick bush, behind which to crouch. I
can see, but cannot be seen.

Father emerges from the thicket.
His voice soars above the swirling
river. "This is the place," he says.

5. CLAY MAN

Father lights the torches and places them around a clear patch of the riverbank. The flames illuminate the place where my dream led me a week ago. My father then draws a shape in the damp ground with the point of a stick. He points to the river. Again, he leads the way and is the first to reach the water.

The men fall to their knees; their pale hands gather great clumps of red clay, just as I did in my dream. They carry it back to the marked space, molding and shaping the clay as though making bread.

My fingers remember the touch of the wet clay. It takes all my willpower to stop myself from running to join them.

When they finish, they rise and look at what they have made. Lying flat and still on the ground is a man of clay.

Father walks around him, whispering words I cannot understand, then turns to Isaac and Uncle Samuel. Isaac walks in a circle seven times from right to left. I count each one on my fingers. Father speaks, clearly now, words of strange power. The clay body begins to glow like the embers of a fire. I can feel the heat rising, warming the air, reaching me in my hiding place.

Next, Uncle Samuel begins his walk, also in a circle around the shape seven times from right to left, chanting phrases also unknown to me. A mist rises from the ground, quenching the fire. The shape moves, trembles as I do, for I see hair growing on its head. The red body, no longer clay, becomes flesh and skin; nails grow on its feet and fingers. It looks like a man.

I am not supposed to be here to witness this mystery, but how can I look away? Father traces a word upon the stranger's forehead: the letters glow brightly. The word remains there for only a moment, then pales, fading away as though it had never been. But I saw the word *EMET*, which I know means "truth." *Is this the "truth" that Father said he was searching for?*

Father speaks again, his voice as clear as if he were speaking in the synagogue: "'And the Lord God formed man of the dust of the ground, and breathed into his nostrils the breath of life; and man became a living soul.'"

Father, Isaac, and Uncle Samuel bow to North and South, to East and West, all the corners of the universe. Father places something into the mouth of the man, whose eyes open and look only at him.

I crawl as close as I dare, hoping to hear more.

"This parchment I have placed between your lips bears the *Shem*, the name of the One who created the world. Get up," Father says, reaching his hand out to help.

The clay man stands – he is the tallest man I have ever seen.

Now I remember the words I heard Father speak on the night of my dream: "I must make a golem."

Is this man a golem? If so, then Father is indeed a magician.

Isaac takes clothes from the bundle he brought. Then he and Uncle Samuel dress the golem.

"I am Rabbi Judah Loew, your master. I name you Josef. You will live in my home and do as I tell you. You must obey only me. I have created you out of the earth . . . formed you of fire, water, and air.

"This has been done for a single purpose – to protect our people, the Jews. You must do no harm, yet make sure that we Jews are not harmed by our enemies.

"You are like other men, yet not the same. You can see and hear more than others and go where ordinary men cannot go. Unlike men, you cannot speak. If you understand me, bow you head."

The golem bows.

"Good, now it is time to leave."

I HURRY AWAY; I must get home before them. I hear
Father, Isaac, Uncle Samuel, and the golem stumbling
behind me. When I reach the ghetto walls, I turn
around and glimpse the four figures in the distance –
four, when a few hours ago there were only three.

I scramble through the gap and am home and in
my bed before Father returns.

My last thought before I fall asleep is to wonder if
this night has all been a dream. . . .

6. JOSEF

I wake to the sounds of clattering pots and my baby sister's chatter. I must have slept late. I dress hurriedly and go down to the kitchen, not certain if last night really happened.

"How did you graze your cheek, Jacob?" Mother asks, spooning food into Rebecca's mouth.

I put my hand to my face. "I don't know, Mother. It doesn't hurt."

Father comes in, followed by a man so tall that he must stoop to walk through the kitchen doorway. I recognize him instantly, and yet here inside our house, he looks different altogether: a face formed crookedly, one dark eye bigger than the other, a gash for a mouth.

I speak to him in my thoughts: *I dreamt of you, Clay Man, but the river washed you away before you were finished. I am glad to see you whole. I saw you brought to life, and this time the river did not take you from me.*

We are used to having visitors at all times in our home – the rabbi's house is where everyone is sent who has nowhere else to go. Father tells Josef to sit on the stool by the hearth. The stranger moves slowly, sits staring straight ahead.

"This is Josef," Father tells us. "I have hired him to assist Avraham, our synagogue servant, with his duties. He will help the old man to keep the lamps clean and lit at all times, watch over the premises, and perform any other tasks for our community that I think are suitable."

Mother asks, "Where is he from, Judah? Surely he's not from the ghetto? I have never seen him before, and I know everyone who lives here."

"I found him wandering the streets late last night, lost in the dark. He could tell me nothing, for he is unable to utter a single word, poor mute creature. Yet he understands everything. He will live here with us," Father says.

"You are welcome, Josef." Mother begins to slice bread. "You may earn your breakfast by chopping wood for the stove." She smiles at him, but Josef does not seem to notice or to have heard her.

"Pearl," Father says, "I have not brought Josef home to do our household chores. Each day, I will find him tasks to benefit all who live in the ghetto. Please remember, I am the only one who may give him orders. Jacob, have you finished your breakfast? Josef and I will walk partway to school with you."

Passersby stare at the huge figure of Josef walking. They shrink away, uneasy about the tall stranger in our midst.

"Work hard, my son. Don't let your thoughts wander," Father says. *Has the teacher been telling tales about me?* Father beckons to Josef, and they walk through the great doors into the Old-New Synagogue.

I TRY TO PAY ATTENTION in *cheder*, but schoolwork seems dull compared to all that has happened in our family these last few days. Father wants me to study hard, but how can I? I am too busy thinking about Josef, trying to remember exactly how he came to be.

Josef was in my dream first, but I had no time to complete him. *Did I really see Father create him? If I had finished making my clay man, would he have walked and talked?* I shall try to teach him to say my name . . . I will be friends with him, if he lets me. . . .

"Jacob Loew, I have twice called upon you to read. Is it too much to ask the rabbi's son to pay attention in class?" The teacher raps his pointer on the table. "You will stay late after school for extra study."

When at last he lets me go, I run down Klausen Street past the old prayer house, along the narrow alley behind Pinkas Synagogue. There, I turn into a wider lane. I will soon be home.

I see Josef walking a short distance ahead of me. For the first time, I notice that he limps. I'll catch up with him, so we can walk back home together.

7. "Not like other men"

I call out to him, "Josef, wait for me!" but he turns the corner without looking round. When I follow, he has gone, disappeared. *How can he vanish when all the doors are shut?* It's as if the ground has opened up and swallowed him.

By the time I reach home a few minutes later, he is there before me, sitting by the kitchen hearth as if he has been there for hours.

"Didn't you hear me call you, Josef? I wanted to walk home with you."

Mother comes bustling in, carrying her empty basket.

"Kept in again, Jacob? I've been waiting for you to get home. Supper will be late if the water kegs aren't filled. Take the buckets to the well. I'll be back as soon as I pick up the herrings from the fishmonger. Hurry, please, before your father comes home wanting his supper."

Once she leaves, I decide to ask Josef to go instead. *Why not?* He's much bigger and faster than I am.

"Josef, the kegs are almost empty. Mother needs

water to cook supper. Please fill these buckets at
the well."

He gets up and does as I ask, returning much more
quickly than I could have done. I watch him pour the
water from the buckets into the kegs, glad that my
idea has worked so well. I go upstairs, thinking how
pleased Mother will be on her return.

"JACOB, HELP! Stop it, Josef, that's enough water!"
Mother screams.

I rush downstairs. Water spills down the sides of
the overflowing kegs. Rebecca sits in a puddle that
is spreading over the kitchen floor. She splashes
and plays with the herrings Mother has dropped
in her panic.

I shout, "Stop, Josef! You have brought enough water – the kegs are full. Are you trying to drown us?"

He doesn't listen, but goes back to the well, returning with two more buckets, full to the brim. The minute he starts to empty them, Mother and I grab his arms, but he shakes us off as easily as a horse swishes away two bothersome flies. The water continues to rise.

Our neighbors gather to stare and to shout advice, but the moment Josef has emptied the buckets, he goes right back to the well. *Will he never stop? Why doesn't he obey us?*

Rebecca crows with joy, which turns to a piercing scream when Mother picks her up and hands her, dripping, to Mrs. Feldman from next door.

In the uproar, Father appears.

"Stop, Josef!" he commands him. "Put down the buckets and wait outside until I call you."

Josef obeys instantly.

"I met Josef coming from the well and heard the commotion. Who told him to fetch water? I thought I made it clear that I am the only one who may tell Josef what to do." Father looks stern.

"It is my fault, Father. I asked Josef to fetch the water. I'm sorry. Mother asked me to do it, but I was tired."

"Tired? That is not what your school teacher said about you. I will tell you once more: Josef is not here to take over anyone's chores, least of all those of a boy who comes home late because he has been kept in after school for not paying attention. Josef was sent to the ghetto to protect our community – to keep us safe from our enemies. He is not to do anything that might keep him from that. Do you understand?"

Sent? What is Father talking about? Josef was not "sent." Didn't I see Father make him from lumps of clay?

"Yes, Father. But why did he obey me when I first asked him and then refuse to stop when the kegs were full?"

"Enough of your questions, Jacob," Mother says. "You have made me late with your father's supper." She pushes a mop into my hand. "Dry this floor please."

"Can I not make you understand, Jacob?" Father says. "Josef is not here to help with household tasks or your chores. He has other, more important duties to fulfill. Josef is not like other men – he does not think or reason as you and I do. He is strong and will protect us from those who tell lies about us . . . who wish us harm. Josef has special gifts, but I am the only one who may decide how and when his gifts will be used. He recognizes that I am his master.

Never disobey me in this way again. Now, help
your mother."

"I will remember. I'm sorry, Father." I dry the floor.

I WISH I KNEW what was going on in Josef's head.
*What does he think about? When he vanished today, did he
make himself invisible? Is that one of his gifts?*

Father did not say that I must stay away from
Josef, only that I must not tell him what to do. He
did not say that I must not watch where he goes in
the ghetto, nor walk beside him, nor stop from
wondering who he really is!

It takes me a long time to mop the floor. *Would it
have mattered, just this once, if Josef had used those special
gifts of his to dry the floor?*

8. "No smoke without fire"

Every week I have to go to market to help Mother carry home the shopping. I never see other boys of my age there. If only Rebecca were old enough to go instead of me! Even cheder is preferable to this!

If I knew how to make myself disappear the way Josef does, I'd do it this minute. My cheeks ache from being pinched by our neighbors. *Oh, no! Mother's stopping again.*

"Good afternoon, Rebbetzin. My, your Jacob is getting tall, but don't you think he's a bit too thin? How old are you now, Jacob? It seems only yesterday that you were learning to walk."

I turn my face into Mother's shawl to avoid another pinch.

"Does he bring home good marks from cheder as his brother used to do?"

"Every child is different," Mother says. "How is your Aaron getting on in the yeshiva?"

Mrs. Kaufman tugs my ear and tries to answer Mother. She can hardly make herself heard above the noise in the square: cackling geese, quacking ducks, women gossiping and comparing prices or the size of cabbages and turnips. Thankfully today I am spared having to listen to Aaron's many accomplishments because something unusual is happening at the dairy stall.

Mother waves to her friend Mrs. Jacobi, who is standing in line, waiting to be served. The women make way for the rabbi's wife. I have to be better behaved as her son and the son of the rabbi, but it does come in useful sometimes.

"What is going on, Mrs. Jacobi? Poor Mrs. Levi looks quite upset," Mother says.

"Some woman has accused Mrs. Levi of cheating. She says she's been shortchanged."

"I don't believe it for one minute!" Mother exclaims.

Mrs. Levi's cheeks are bright red with shame.

The woman, whose clothes do not have our familiar yellow circle sewn on them, shrieks louder than a chicken about to be slaughtered: "You Jews are all the same – cheats and liars! It's as I've always said, 'There's no smoke without fire.' No wonder Emperor Rudolf had to build walls and lock the gates around your dirty little town. It's to keep thieves like you away from us honest, decent folk."

"Mrs. Levi is a good person – a hardworking widow doing her best to make a living for her family.

I'd like to give that woman a piece of my mind. Someone has to, but don't breathe a word to your father," Mother whispers in my ear.

"I won't, but he'll hear about it anyway," I say.

"Go back where you came from!" Mother calls out fiercely. "We don't need strangers calling us bad names in front of our children. This is a peaceful neighborhood, or was, until you showed up."

"I'll not move one step until I get the money I'm owed. My husband warned me not to come here, but my good nature overcame me," the woman replies.

The stranger leans both elbows on the edge of the stall. She's a big heavy woman, and the weight of her body causes the merchandise to slide around.

Mrs. Levi undoes the leather pouch she wears around her waist and takes out some coins. "You asked for six eggs, and I gave you six eggs. You paid for them and pocketed your change. But here you are, take your money back. Let's call it a gesture of goodwill to a visitor to our ghetto. And in future, please buy your eggs in your own city market."

The woman grabs the money and mutters, "Oh, so you admit you shortchanged me? Don't you dare tell me what to do. Warning me off, are you? Well, don't be surprised if one day your stall meets with an accident. No one gets away with insulting me!" She gives the stall a vicious push.

Suddenly Josef appears by her side. He covers her wrist with his big hand.

The woman screams, "Help, a monster has burned my arm!" She rubs her wrist.

The crowd is silent. Josef's arms drop to his side and he stands as still as gravestone. He looks down at the woman and stares into her eyes.

She looks away, fumbling for some coins. "Here, take back your money. I was mistaken." She throws the coins at Mrs. Levi so that they roll off the counter and turns away, pushing through the watching women. Then she hurries out of the market as if every demon in Bohemia were chasing her.

Josef follows a few steps behind her, stronger and more powerful than any ogre she could imagine. The women clap and laugh. They line up again to purchase their cheese, milk, butter, and eggs.

Mrs. Levi carefully arranges twelve beautiful brown eggs in Mother's basket. "With my thanks, no charge. Take it, Rebbetzin – a gift! We are all better off because you and the rabbi have opened your home to Josef. He is a fine man, the more so for not having a tongue to argue with."

Mother and Mrs. Levi look at each other, and the women roar with laughter. *What is so funny?* Mother thanks Mrs. Levi and we go home, Mother still smiling. Sometimes, I don't understand her.

THAT EVENING after supper, I go up to Josef sitting by the hearth and touch his hand. It feels as though he has just taken it out of a basin of cold water. *How could he have burned that woman's hand?*

He can disappear . . . make people think they are hurt when they are not. *Are these the special gifts Father was talking about?*

9. A Wedding Feast

A storm has been raging for two whole days. Great gusts of wind rattle the shutters, howl through cracks and under doors. It rains day and night, and the water flows down the gutters in torrents.

Mother keeps me home from school today because yesterday at cheder, I sat all day in my damp clothes. I coughed the whole night. She rubs goose grease on my chest. I don't mind the stench, if it means I can spend the day at home by the fire.

Mrs. Feldman's daughter Sarah is to be married tomorrow, and the entire street has been invited to the feast. Mother is making noodle pudding with chopped nuts to bring to the celebration. Her hands are deep in flour. Meanwhile, she murmurs comforting words to Minnie Feldman, who sits crying at the kitchen table, her tears leaving watery streaks on the floury surface.

"Pearl, what am I to do? The fishermen cannot go out in this storm. There is not a fish left to buy at the stalls, not so much as a single herring anywhere in the ghetto. I was promised a fine big carp – enough for all the guests. Now there won't be sufficient food. My Sarah will be shamed in front of her new in-laws."

Mother attempts to soothe her. "Dry your tears, Minnie. Everyone will bring something, you'll see. And you can serve your famous apple pancakes. No one will even notice there is no fish!"

Mrs. Feldman refuses to be comforted. "You know as well as I do that according to tradition, I must serve carp." She dabs at her tears with the corner of her apron. "Pearl, a favor, I beg of you," she pleads, looking at Josef sitting on his stool.

I can guess what the favor is.

"Just this one time, lend me your Josef. He can do anything – everyone says so. He's as strong as . . . well, strong enough to go fishing even in this terrible storm."

"I'm sorry, Minnie," Mother says. "I promised Judah, who insists that we must never take Josef away from his duties."

"What duties? Sitting by a nice warm fire while I worry myself to death? Here, Josef, I brought my grain sack. Take it, go to the river, and fill it with carp. I need enough fish for the wedding feast." Mrs. Feldman puts the sack in Josef's hand.

He is up and is out of the house before Mother has a chance to tell him to stay.

44

I run to the door. "Come back, Josef!" I shout, even though I know it's useless.

Mother calls too, at the top of her voice, waving her rolling pin as if that would make him turn back. But the wind is so strong, her words get lost and the door slams shut. By the time we open it again, Josef has disappeared from our street.

"I am so grateful, Pearl," Mrs. Feldman says. "I'll go back to my preparations now. Just send Jacob over with the fish when Josef returns."

As soon as she leaves, Mother says, "She doesn't understand – her head is full of wedding plans. I must find your father and explain what has happened. After all he told us and our promise to him . . . no good can come of this. Josef will fish until there's not a fish left in the river if your father doesn't order him to stop. Stay here and look after Rebecca."

She does not need to remind me of the day I asked Josef to fetch water from the well. *Who knows what he is up to now?* "I can go, Mother. My cough is almost better. Let me go instead."

"Don't argue with me, Jacob! I shall go." She throws her shawl over her head, fastens it tightly, and runs out into the rain, slamming the door behind her.

After a while, she returns and hangs her shawl near the fire to dry.

"Father is attending a meeting, but I asked Avraham to send him home along the river the moment he is free. I told him the matter is urgent. All we can do is hope he won't be long."

She rolls out dumplings for tonight's chicken soup.

There is a knock at the door, and Mother asks me to answer it.

"Pearl, my worries are over!" Mrs. Feldman cries. "The fishmonger brought over a carp – not as big as I'd hoped, but big enough. Don't ask me where he got it. He didn't tell me and I don't care. So, my dear Pearl, Jacob can tell Josef to come home. Don't worry about the sack – you can bring it tomorrow. And thank you, Pearl, for putting up with me." She races off.

FATHER RETURNS later than usual, but I am relieved to see Josef with him. The moment Mother hears Father's step, she drops the dumplings into the soup to simmer. Josef goes to his place by the hearth.

"I am sorry, Judah," Mother says. "But nothing stops Minnie Feldman when her mind is made up. She asked Josef to go to the river for carp before I had a chance to say no. I did try."

"How hard did you and Jacob try, Pearl?" Father asks.

I cough, so I don't have to answer. Father starts laughing and, a moment later, Mother joins in.

"What else is a poor rabbi to do? I should cry, but to laugh is better. Remember that, when you become a rabbi, Jacob." He wipes his eyes. "This time no harm has been done. When I reached the river, Josef was standing waist-high in water, a carp under his chin, its tail slapping his face. The sack was full to bursting. When I told him to stop fishing, he emptied the sack into the water and threw the carp back after it.

"I will talk to the congregation this week. I will explain that no one may keep Josef from his duties, which are only to watch over us and our ghetto. I should have done so before. It is especially important as the festival of Passover approaches."

At the wedding celebration the next day, Father tells Mrs. Feldman she has prepared a feast fit for Emperor Rudolf himself. I think Mother's chicken soup tastes better than any old carp!

10. "Poison"

Father has barely finished saying his morning prayers and the baker is already waiting to see him.

"Rebbe, forgive me for disturbing you so early. I am in urgent need of your help."

"Please come in, Mr. Bloch. Jacob, stir up the fire. How can I be of help to you? My baking skills, I'm afraid, are not as great as my wife's."

"You joke, Rebbe, but I am facing an emergency. Did you hear about my partner, Nachum? He has had an accident and is unable to come to work for a few days. I will fall behind with Passover orders. We had only just begun to prepare the matzos."

"Baker Block, how serious can a few days be? You can hire someone for a short time."

"I need someone today, if possible. Believe me, I've made inquiries, but no one has come forward, at least not from the ghetto."

"However, I am right that there is a 'however'?" Father says.

"Indeed you are right, Rebbe. The 'however' is

naturally subject to your approval. There is a baker in the old city – a good man who runs a well-established business. I approached him, and he suggested that he spare one of his own apprentices for a few days. He feels it would be valuable experience, for one learning the art, to observe our way of baking.

"It is just until Nachum can return. The apprentice, Boris, will do odd jobs, help wait on the customers, take orders. Only I will prepare the matzos – he would not go near the mixing. Would there be an objection, Rebbe?"

"It is not against the law, Baker Bloch, so hire him with a clear conscience. But, I have a 'however' too. I should like to meet this young man who is not from the ghetto."

"He is waiting outside, Rebbe."

"Jacob, show the young man in, please."

A tall skinny apprentice enters, and Father greets him pleasantly. Mr. Bloch tells Boris to show Father his hands. The young man wipes them on his apron before spreading his fingers wide for Father to inspect. Then he turns them palm upwards. His hands look a lot cleaner than mine!

Josef comes over from his corner by the hearth and stands behind Father. Boris shifts from one foot to the other, staring at the floor.

"So, Boris, how do you feel about working in the

Jewish town for a while?" Father asks.

"It is an honor, sir," he replies.

"Then I wish you both good day. Go in peace."

They turn to leave, but Josef takes one big stride and bars their way.

"Come, come, Josef, let us pass. We have much work to do," says the baker, impatient to be gone.

Josef stands aside and lets them leave. But the moment they reach the street, he grabs Boris by the collar, tosses him into the air, brings him down again, only to spin him round and round as if he were a top.

"Help, help!" Boris cries. Shutters open. Faces peer around doors.

"Josef, are you crazy? Rebbe, I beg you, tell him to stop," the baker pleads.

"Stop, Josef!" Father calls out.

Josef lets the young man go, and he falls in a shivering heap to the ground.

"I have done nothing, nothing . . . ," he whimpers.

"That we shall soon find out," Father says.

Josef drags Boris to his feet. He removes a small flask filled with colorless liquid from Boris's jacket pocket. Father takes it, removes the stopper, and sniffs. He passes the flask to the baker. Boris tries to slink off, but Josef grips his shoulder, stopping him.

The baker's face is pale. "Poison," he whispers. "I dare not think how easy it would have been for this evil youth to pour a few drops into the matzo flour while my back was turned. He has deceived me, Rebbe. If it was not for your good Josef, all our Passover matzos would have been contaminated. How many of us might have fallen sick or died?"

"Good riddance, I say," Boris mutters.

"Jacob, you will be late," Father says. "Your teacher will have just cause to complain again. Off you go.

"My dear Mr. Bloch, you and Josef and I will take this vagabond to the magistrate in the old city. He will know how to deal with him."

When Father comes home in the evening, he hands Mother a gift from our baker – a freshly baked, braided *challa*.

"Aren't you going to tell us what happened at the magistrate's court, Father?" (I could think of nothing else all day in cheder!)

"Boris confessed that a fellow worker, who bore a grudge against Jews, paid him to poison the matzos. The baker fired them both, and Boris was given a big fine to pay by the magistrate.

"Mr. Bloch says if he has to work day and night, it is not important as long as everyone in the ghetto has their Passover matzos in time."

11. The Blood Lie

oday our teacher lets us out early from school. He tells us to go home and study for tomorrow's test. But, instead, I walk to the gates of the ghetto, hoping that Josef is still there, as he is most days, guarding us. He is taller and stronger than anyone in the whole of Prague!

This is the busiest part of the day – early afternoon – a time when women from outside the ghetto enter, looking for bargains: the best cloth, the biggest eggs, the finest plucked chickens. We see peddlers and Gypsies, travelers, tradesmen, and merchants, all searching to buy or sell in the hours before dusk . . . in the hours before the gates are locked.

Josef looks at those entering: *Do they wish to harm us? Are there pickpockets or thieves among them? Those ready to accuse us falsely and spread untruths or evil rumors?*

Passover approaches and Father reminds Josef daily to be extra vigilant. This is why Josef stands, hour after hour, watching all who come and go. He is still there, and I stand beside him, waiting for him to begin another round of the ghetto. He walks at odd times, even in darkness when doors are shut tight.

Sometimes I see his shadow passing by, magnified by the last flicker of the candles before they are extinguished and I fall asleep.

Are the night demons and ghosts, which hover over the sloping roofs, frightened away by Josef? He makes me feel safe. No corner is too dark for him to peer around, no wall too high for him to climb, no alleyway too narrow for him to pass through.

Walking beside him this afternoon, I take notice of how he listens to the slightest sound. He seems to become part of the air, of the stones we walk on, of the crooked doors, the crumbling entranceways. He knows the hidden paths and inner courtyards better than I do, and I have been exploring them ever since I was a small boy and Mother allowed me the freedom of the ghetto.

Nothing escapes him. Footsteps that do not belong to a ghetto dweller make him pause. A cry muted by the mournful singing of men at prayer, or muffled by the sound of children playing, transforms him into the stillness of a headstone in the graveyard. He looks fearsome to those who do not know him, but we who live here have become accustomed to his presence in our midst.

As we walk, I tell Josef things about the ghetto. I feel he listens and understands.

"That is the house of David Gans, the astronomer. He studies the movement of the stars. Do you ever watch the sky, Josef?"

Often I forget that Josef will never answer me . . . will never say my name. I am used to the way he disappears, even as I am talking to him. I still have not managed to discover how he does it.

I think of him as my friend. But a little while ago, Father reminded me, "Remember, Jacob, Josef is not like us. He has no soul."

I did not disagree, but when Mother lights the candles on Friday evening, I see Josef's eyes change. They become gentle . . . as kind as Father's when he gives us his blessing. I almost believe Josef smiles. I hope he can stay with us always. I think Father is mistaken. He does not understand Josef as I do.

WE REACH THE CENTER, the most crowded part of the ghetto. An apothecary shop stands at the corner; next to it is an inn. A silversmith, a shoemaker, a printer, and a toolmaker jostle for space side by side further up the lane. Two or three families live in each of the dwellings.

Micah, a friend from school, lives in this part of the ghetto. Once, when I went to his home to play, he showed me an underground passage from his cellar leading all the way under the houses in the lane. We followed the route until it ended at Mayor Maisel's town hall and synagogue.

Micah thinks I'm lucky the chief rabbi is my father. He is envious because we do not have to share our home with other families. I tell him about the people who come to visit Father at all hours seeking advice – the travelers that eat with us most every meal, or stay for nights. Often I give up my bed to them.

I peer into the window of the apothecary at the narrow shelves holding rows of bottles and flasks of colored liquids. There are jars of mysterious powders and boxes of salves and ointments.

A horse whinnies; a cart trundles to a stop. The driver pats his horse's neck and unloads a bundle wrapped in sacking. He goes round the back into the courtyard to make his delivery. The horse lowers its head to the cobblestones, picks up a vegetable rind, and eats greedily. I am hungry and look around for Josef to tell him I am going home, but he has vanished into the cold gray air.

The driver returns, his hands bound with rope. Josef towers behind him, looking somehow as if he has grown! He carries the sack as tenderly as if it contained my baby sister. *Whatever is in it?* The driver does not cry out for help. His face is white and fearful. *Did the man try to steal something?*

Josef places the sack into the cart and throws the driver after it just as though he were a trussed chicken. He ties his feet together and takes the driver's seat.

"Josef, wait for me!" I call, but he drives off and I'm forced to run behind. I try to keep up, but the cart goes too fast. Josef has forgotten all about me. . . .

AFTER SUPPER, Father tells us the story.

"This afternoon Josef discovered a man in the ghetto attempting to conceal the body of a child in the cellar beneath the town hall. It is what I feared might happen one day. The little boy, younger than you, Jacob, was ready for burial. If the man had succeeded in his evil plan, we would have been tainted once again with the Blood Lie: the murder of a Christian child for the purpose of using his blood in our Passover matzos.

"We drove out of the ghetto and brought the culprit to the chief of police. The man confessed. It seems a priest had ordered him to do this. Both are in prison and will no doubt remain there for a long time."

Mother starts to cry.

"Don't cry, Mother, it is all over now," I tell her.

"Jacob, I weep for the child's parents. I shall remember them in my prayers," she says. "Judah, I bless the day you found Josef and brought him to this house."

12. "To save a life"

———✦———

Three years have passed since Josef came to live among us. We have celebrated our festivals without fear because of his presence. His eyes and ears are everywhere, allowing nothing and no one to harm us. Those enemies outside our walls that tried to plot and scheme were discovered. Not one of them succeeded.

Word spread rapidly in Prague and throughout Bohemia that it was better not to plot against the Jews. Also, Emperor Rudolf admires our learning and looks unfavorably on those that try to blacken our reputation.

I am almost thirteen and will soon take my place with the men in the synagogue. Next year, I will leave cheder and study at the yeshiva. There will be less time to walk with Josef . . . less time to explore and play with my friends. Still I have not found the courage to talk to Father about my dreams for the future. I shall do so soon and hope that he understands. I do not want him to be disappointed in me.

The week is nearly over. It is late on Friday

afternoon and the Sabbath approaches. Mother has covered the supper table with a white cloth and set out her best dishes. The house is filled with the smell of roasting chicken; two freshly baked challas stand by the silver candlesticks. I can almost taste the sweet white bread and wish the sun would hurry up and set.

Every Friday, before the start of the Sabbath, Father reminds Josef of his duties. From sunset on Friday to sunset on Saturday, he may walk and keep watch over the ghetto, for Josef is not bound as we are to keep our Sabbath laws. But once the Sabbath begins, Father cannot break our law by giving him any further instructions.

My sister hops from one leg to the other, anxious for the best meal of the week.

Mother has changed into her good dress and waits for Father to come home. "Go and see what is keeping your father, Jacob. The service is over; all the men are on their way home. It is almost time for me to light the candles. Whatever can be delaying him? And Josef, too, has not been home today."

I run over to the synagogue. Avraham is about to shut the heavy doors. He calls out to me, "Your father said to tell you that he has been called to the bedside of a sick child. He will be home as soon as he can."

The street is quiet. Everyone is already in their homes, ready to welcome the Sabbath evening. I walk a little farther, hoping to meet Josef. He has never missed the candle-lighting. I will bring him back with me if I see him.

JOSEF IS AT the ghetto gates, not quiet and watchful as usual, but pacing back and forth. He waves his arms and kicks at the wall. There is menace in his movements.

On the eve of this Sabbath, Josef is fearsome to behold. He rattles and shakes the gates, which are locked, with such force that I am afraid he may tear them from their foundations. *What has disturbed him?*

A small crowd gathers on the other side of the wall.

"Look at the Jewish giant," a man calls out.

"He has gone mad," someone whispers.

"Will he destroy us all?" another shouts.

"You'd better keep to your own side of the wall," a workman says, putting down his bag of tools and rolling up his sleeves.

The crowd is agitated and murmurs angrily.

If only Father were here, he would know how to calm Josef down.

"Josef, come home with me now," I say, going to stand close beside him.

The crowd jostles for a better view. Josef raises an empty cart into the air and brings it crashing down on the wall. It splinters into pieces. Josef brandishes two staves wrenched from the broken cart, hitting out at everything before him. The blows narrowly miss the fingers of the man grasping the edge of the wall. The man slinks away and the others follow, afraid of what Josef will do next.

I am afraid too. *What has made him behave like this?* He was our protector and now he has become a stranger. I try again to coax him to leave.

"Come home, Josef. Mother is ready to light the candles."

He loves to watch her, but today he shakes me off – unseeing, unhearing, running in circles before he turns down a side street, kicking walls and beating at doors.

I run for home; I cannot make him stop. I do not have power over a golem bent on destruction. Only Father can help us.

I collide with him outside the synagogue.

"Jacob, my son, I was delayed. Your mother will be anxious. If we hurry, we can still reach home in time."

"No, Father, we cannot go home. Josef is possessed! You have to stop him! He will kill someone." I take Father's arm and we follow the terrible sounds of a wooden club thudding against doors and shutters. Father's lips move in prayer.

We approach Josef. He looms, a great shadow outlined against the last rays of the setting sun. Josef readies his cudgel to shatter a nearby window.

Father raises his eyes to the sky. "The sun has set. I am too late. The Sabbath has arrived."

I seize the hem of Josef's coat to distract him, but suddenly he lifts me high over his head. *Will he smash me down on the cobbles – splinter me into pieces like the wooden cart?*

Father cries out: "Stop, Josef! Come to me."

Immediately Josef calms. He sets me gently on my feet. His arms drop to his sides.

"Come, Josef, we are going home." Father's voice is steady, quiet.

We walk on either side of Josef, our path lit by the flames of Sabbath candles shining through windows and cracks in shutters. Families are gathered around their supper table. Only we are late. Father has broken our law. *For me?* Not a word is spoken until we are inside the house.

FATHER SAYS, "Sit down in your place, Josef," and Josef sits.

Mother serves the meal in silence. She has lit the candles and spoken the blessing without us. I find it hard to swallow my food.

"To save a life, one may break a commandment. Will I break our Holy Law for a broken shutter, a window? No. But for my son, for a life in danger, it is permitted. Josef's strength is that of ten men. I am to blame – I forgot to remind him of his Sabbath duties. Without any instructions to follow, he did not know what to do. He became a crazed being, unable to distinguish between right and wrong."

We struggle to finish our meal. I have never known a Friday night when we were not joyful to be together.

Now we are saddened by what has happened. Even Rebecca understands that this Sabbath is different from any that has gone before.

13. "He is only sleeping"

———✤———

The Sabbath crawls by. Josef remains seated in the kitchen. We attend services in the synagogue as usual, but Father's sermon and the familiar prayers are not enough to unravel the tight knot of unhappiness inside me.

How can I forget the moment when Josef treated me as an enemy? I thought he understood that I am his friend. Father said he is not like us, and I didn't want to believe him. I won't believe him. It was a mistake, and we will go on as we did before.

At the midday meal, Mother's *cholent* – the stew of meat and beans she prepares for us before the start of the Sabbath – today tastes no better than ashes on my tongue.

When everyone is out of the kitchen except for Josef, I stand facing him, hoping he will look at me. He will not, but continues to stare at the floor almost as if he were ashamed.

I say, "Father is not angry with you, Josef. He said he was to blame. You heard him, didn't you? Look at me, Josef. We are still friends, you and I." He does not move.

The sun goes down at last. Never before have I felt relief that the Sabbath is over. The sky is clear tonight. The first three stars appear one by one and now more, too many to count, as many as my questions that Father has not answered. *How will I ever go to sleep?*

The house settles down for the night. Father is in his study. I hear him pulling books down from the shelf, sigh, turn the pages. Then a long silence. I go in to say good night.

"You cannot sleep either, Jacob? It has been a difficult time for us all, but at last I have reached a decision. You and I and Josef will walk to the Old-New Synagogue. I will tell Josef he is to sleep there tonight. We will go now, quietly, so as not to disturb your mother."

I do not question Father, but wonder what decision he has come to.

THE THREE OF US walk through the silent streets. Everything reminds me of that long-ago night when I followed Father to the river. I am no longer afraid of spirits and demons, but of something that is about to end.

We enter the Old-New Synagogue through a side door, partially hidden by leafy branches. Father bolts it once we are inside. He lights a candle stub and we climb up the narrow winding staircase to the top. Father unlocks the door of an attic room under the gables. I have never been up here before.

"Wait here, Josef," Father says. He motions me to help him clear a heap of parchments, threadbare prayer shawls, and worn books that cover a narrow couch at the far end of the room.

"Lie down, Josef," Father commands. Josef obeys at once. Father removes the Shem, the small piece of parchment on which the name of the Creator is written, from Josef's mouth and speaks to him: "The work for which you were created is finished. You have done well, Josef. You kept us safe from our enemies, and the danger to our people is past. We walk in safety now and sleep peacefully at night, thanks to you. Your time with us has ended." He touches Josef's forehead and on it appears a word: *EMET*. The letters glow briefly in the dim light of the attic.

I have seen this word on his forehead before – the night when the clay man was formed. Father erases the initial letter, *E*, so that the word now spells *MET*, meaning "death."

Death? Is Josef going to die? Is this the decision Father has made? I am filled with terror.

The letters of the word grow pale, fade, and disappear. Josef's eyes close. I want to shout to wake him up, but know this is a sacred moment, one that

I must not disturb.

Father circles the couch seven times from left to right, reversing the way he walked before, when he created the golem from clay. Just like then, I do not understand the words he whispers.

He bows to East and West, to North and South. Josef lies still.

"It is finished," Father says. He motions me to help him cover Josef with prayer shawls and parchments. When we are done, the attic room looks as it did when we entered.

"Father, will you say a *kaddish* for Josef? He was my friend."

"Jacob, you know that the kaddish is a prayer of mourning spoken only for the dead. Josef is not dead – he is only sleeping."

"How long he will he remain asleep? Will he ever awaken and return to the ghetto, Father?"

"One day, when the Jewish people have great need of him, the golem may be called upon again. But, for now, Josef has returned to the earth from which he came."

This time Father's words do not comfort me. In my heart, I know that I will not see Josef again.

"Jacob, do I have your promise that you will never speak of what you have seen and heard here tonight to anyone?"

"I promise." My voice cracks unexpectedly. I am too old to cry.

"If anyone asks where Josef has gone, you must say that he has returned to his home. And now it is time to go." Father leads the way down the stairs. As he unlocks the door, the candle stub flickers and goes out. We step into the silence of the night. Two, when before there were three.

14. "The courage to speak"

～✦～

My thoughts are of Josef, waiting up there in the dark . . . waiting for a voice to call him back to us.

"Let us talk awhile, Jacob," Father says and motions for me to sit with him at the kitchen table.

I am glad not to have to go to bed yet, but I try not to look at Josef's stool standing empty by the hearth. I shall miss him always.

"Tomorrow I have been invited for an audience with the emperor. I have received word from an advisor at the palace that Emperor Rudolf will announce throughout his lands that the Jewish religion forbids the use of animal or human blood. He will proclaim, therefore, that the Blood Lie is false."

"Father, aren't you happy? Now we will be safe forever."

"Yes, I am content. I pray the emperor's reign may endure many years, so that we will continue to live in peace. It is what we all pray for. The Lie has haunted our people far too long. This is a golden age for us, Jacob.

"David Gans tells me that he, too, has been invited to the audience. I am to answer questions on the mysteries of kabbala, and he will speak about his findings on mathematics and astronomy. The emperor is a man of learning and many interests. It is an honor for our community that both of us are to meet with him."

"May I walk with you, Father, just a little way, and wait for you?"

"I have a better idea. Come with me right to the palace and walk around the gardens, which are magnificent. Who knows, you might even be permitted inside the great hall. I should like you to meet David Gans."

I think immediately of what I might say to him. I hear he is looking for a new apprentice. *Has Father really invited me to go with him? I'm not dreaming, am I?*

"Thank you, Father. I never thought or hoped . . ." I stammer with excitement and will never be able to sleep tonight.

"Good, that is settled then. Now, it is time you went to bed."

"May I ask a question before I go, Father?"

"I like to hear your questions, Jacob."

"I don't know how to begin, but it is something that puzzles me. That first morning when you brought Josef to live with us, I felt I knew him. I recognized him, or believed I did.

"I had followed you the night you left the ghetto with Isaac and Uncle Samuel. I hid and watched you make a man out of clay. The night was so dark, even with the brightness of the torches and the moon. Everything I saw and remembered has become confused, mixed up with my own dreams of the clay figure I tried to make. Was it Josef you created, Father?"

"Yes, my son."

"That night you spoke words I could not understand. Were they the same ones you spoke tonight, before Josef fell sleep?"

"All these years you have waited to speak of this night to me. How can a boy keep such a long silence?" My father's eyes are kind.

"You knew I was there?" I am astonished. *How could he know?* "I was so sure no one saw me."

"It was your secret as well as mine," Father says. "I waited for you to tell me. I am glad you have. The night of your dream, you heard me call out and you came into the study. I, too, had been dreaming. For many days, I had been seeking an answer to the problem of how to keep the ghetto safe during Passover. I prayed . . . searched the texts for answers. I fell asleep and, in my dream, the letters flew into the air from the pages of the *Sefer Yezirah*.

"They formed and reformed into different patterns, and then it seemed a voice told me to make a golem in the likeness of a man – one of great strength, obedient only to me. A man created from the clay of the earth, unable to speak, an unfinished being without a soul.

"Once I was awake, I fully understood the words in the book and realized that to make a golem, I would need the four elements: earth, fire, water, air. This is what you saw and heard.

"Tonight, I spoke the words again, but in reverse order, undoing what had been done when I brought Josef to life. The golem's work is finished. I have been reminded that without my instructions, without a cause, he has become a danger to himself and to us . . . I am to blame."

"But you stopped Josef in time. You are a magician, Father."

"No, Jacob, not a magician. I am a student, as you and Shimon and Isaac are. The scriptures contain the answer to my questions and will continue to guide me as long as I live."

Father has given me the courage to speak . . . to tell him what I have been afraid to tell him for so long.

"I am not like you or Shimon, Father. What would you say if I told you that – " I fumble for the right words.

"That you do not wish to become a rabbi?"
Father's question is so unexpected, I become as
mute as Josef was.

"Then I would listen, think a little, and have to
agree with you – two rabbis in one family are enough!
It seems to me that there are many ways to serve our
people. A boy, a young man such as you are now,
who knows how to keep a secret, who is a kind and
honorable friend, and who asks questions, such a
person can become anything he chooses to be.

"Tomorrow you will embark, by daylight this time,
on a journey to discover a world outside the ghetto.
Who knows? You may find that all you have been
searching for is right here. Good night, my son."

If Josef had never come, would all this have been possible?

I fall asleep, grateful for the time Josef spent with
us, and dream of tomorrow.

Afterword

Does the golem wait to be called upon again? Is he still asleep near the rafters of the Old-New Synagogue in Prague? No one knows for sure.

The Jewish ghetto in the story, its inhabitants led by Rabbi Judah Loew, is gone forever. In 1890, the crooked houses, alleys, and courtyards were demolished and replaced by new housing. However, some important sites were saved.

Rabbi Judah Loew (1520–1609) is buried in the Jewish cemetery, as is David Gans (1541–1613) – astronomer, writer, and mathematician. Mayor Maisel (1528–1601), who built the Jewish town hall, also has his gravestone there.

The Old-New Synagogue still holds services for the Jewish community of Prague. The Pinkas and Klausen synagogues are now museums, showing important exhibits of Jewish history in Central Europe.

The ghetto was renamed Josefov in 1784, not after the golem in the story, but in honor of Joseph II, who, like the Holy Roman Emperor Rudolf II (1576–1612), was tolerant of the Jews and granted them some measure of freedom.

Although Rabbi Judah Loew did have a wife called Pearl, Jacob and his neighbors are imaginary.